good deed rain

This is the author's 55th book.
Others include: *Different Planet*,
The Lake Walker, *Kennedy*,
Imaginary Someone, *Florida*,
The Tin Can Telephone,
River Road, *The Trillium Witch*,
and many more...

A
Red Leaf
Boat

A RED LEAF BOAT©2022
Allen Frost, Good Deed Rain
Bellingham, Washington
ISBN 978-1-0879-0066-7

Writing & Leaves: Allen Frost
Cover Production: Priya Shalauta
Quote from *Love in the Afternoon*,
Billy Wilder, 1957.
Apple: TFK!

"What is he, a creature from
outer space?"
    "No. He's an American."

A RED LEAF BOAT

Allen Frost

Good Deed Rain ◊ Bellingham, Washington ◊ 2022

This fall I got a Japanese poncho and rain-pants and rubber boots and decided I would only walk to work. No more riding the bus. No more bicycle. Just me and the ghost of Santoka Taneda. We would take our time and notice things, thoughts that would become these pages. Rain, wind, leaves, apples, cold. I thought I would keep writing these into winter and spring, but this book is stuck in one season, it stopped with the snow.

Red leaf boat origami

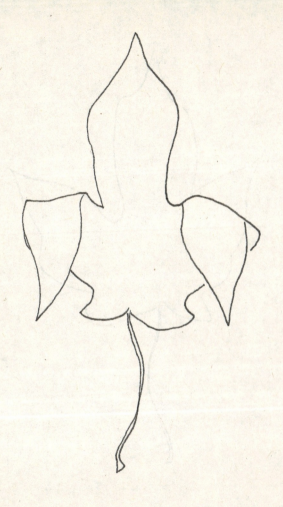

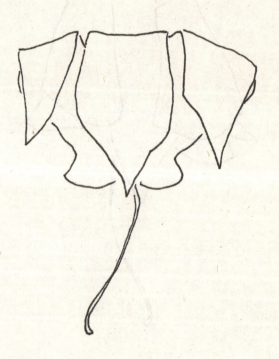

A utility truck
parked by the leaves
both workers busy
eating blackberries

The watchdog
startled by
a butterfly

Deer prints
beside the road
walk with me

Willow tree
long green dream
swim aside

A warm sun
my shadow falls in
with the leaves

Blue jays busy
leaving acorns
in the gutters

Our wind-up dog
awake for a while
then fast asleep

Last night's rain
a full stream below
the wooden bridge

A red leaf boat
sails in the gutter
to the end of a puddle

The wind is back
shaking the colors
off the trees

Empty shell
the sound of wind
blew out the snail

Six leaves
drive from the brush
like yellow taxis

A chainsaw disturbs
the whole world

Leash held tight
a dog propeller
pulls me ahead

Tuning in night
coyote radio

The rabbit bus stop
where they stand in pairs
every day

Disappearing like a candle

Sidewalk tree
holding a sign:
"Don't Pick Plums"

Rain tops
the birdbath
I forgot to fill

Dreams stacked up
against my dark window
like boxcars

Ducks late to work
first they need help
finding the pond

Peaceful
walking inside
morning fog

Every apple
you see in the tree
on sale for free

Beneath the skin
apple worlds
broken by a bite

Thinking about
the names of birds
the junco
for instance

A full moon
stares in the window
too parched to speak

Close to
a certain person
maybe you

A brand-new
morning cobweb
fitted with dew

Real dragons
flying in the wind
half-invisible

Poplars tall as giants

Imagine the farmer
walking along the creek
planting trees long ago

Hear the wind
in the poplar row
running water

Up above me
a raincloud is driving
at my same speed

Hello rainy day
I don't mind being
a frog today

Let the rain
do what it wants
I'm soaked to the skin

Raining there
turn the corner
not raining here

Along the wire
a squirrel escapes

We both stop
to watch the owl
black eyes turning

Light on the lawn
a full moon blossom
in the night sky

Dream rabbits scatter
chased by a sleeping dog

October starts sunny
the leaves hold to the trees
a little longer

The apple tree
waves me over
for breakfast

Dead dragonfly
only the airplane of it
left behind

A mumbling man
steps off the curb
to avoid eye-contact

For a while after a leaf falls
it sits there thinking about
its place in the universe

A tiny oak tree
growing in the path

Rain on leaves is a magic spell
broken by a raven

Trying to map the clouds
everything keeps moving

No time to stop
no apple today
I'm late

Not a bad day
just another day
see what happens

The mushrooms cheer
when I walk by wearing
my wet poncho

Have you noticed
the eyes on trees
they see you too

Carnival crows
five of them
riding the wind

The tree is topped
by red apples
I can't reach

Another leaf
landing beside me
wagging its tail

Forgot paper
I have to write this
on a teabag

It's not just me
someone else carries
a red autumn leaf

A robot voice at work
talking, talking, talking
Ohhh, haunted radio

His car became a house
he cooks dinner on the sidewalk

Light in the kitchen
the other windows asleep

Blue chewing gum
stuck to the roadside
another sign of autumn

Putting a dime
in the slot of a tree
the birds start to sing

Four deer
not the Beatles
cross the road

Halloween masks
fill the steamy windows
a mummy drives the bus

Meeting him again
the mumbling man
he knows me now

In still moments
I hear water running
below the city

Spider web
a telephone wire
waiting for a call

A cold sunflower
shrugs and wonders
where's summer?

Tomato
catching some sun
on the windowsill

The first to walk
in the forest today
I'm covered in dew

Rabbit motorcycle
gone up the hill
in front of me

A deer chewing
my same breakfast
a red apple

Rain drops
small enough to thread
a sewing needle

Followed by ravens
one on a lamppost
another on a fir

I pay more attention to the rain
when I'm getting wet in it

Mushroom pickers
watching the ground
carrying baskets

I surprise them
as I turn the corner
made of trees

Rain on leaves
even with a hole
in my shoe
I stop to listen

Another train of geese flying south
calling out windows to each other

Picked an apple at deer height
the other side is all one bite

A spot to sit
birds and the soft
crashlanding of leaves

The owl has time
to turn the record over
and play the other side
now it's night

Raspberries
picked this morning
with the rain

That leaf knows
where it belongs
look at it go

This poncho
rain-soaked ghost
covers me

A dry junco
using the leaves
for an umbrella

Cars are boats
the street is a river
a sailor's life

Puddles form
in every dip and dent

Looking up
to see a raven
a fat drop of rain
hits my face

Every morning
she drives him to work
kiss and close door

Be careful
worms are on the tar
bathing in rain

Basho's frog
hears a pond
and falls in

Flowers on
the custodian's
blue umbrella

Leafblower
scatters the pattern
made of leaves

Electric deer
short-circuit stagger
across the street

The last living dragonfly
at the end of October, between
a madrona and the sea

They waited until every apple was red
then they picked them all by moonlight

White grass
grown old
from the cold

My hands tell tragic headlines
"Mittens Left at Home"

A morning cloud
in the open field
still sleeping

I walk among the leaves
they're all different, a city
fallen down

The rabbit is new at this
running in circles before finding
the hole in the fence

I'm writing this
underneath a willow
while it's raining

Our friend
the unicyclist
everyone wave!

Resting
a wheelbarrow
in the woods

Winter scouts move in at night
leaving ice on the windows

Stories spill into the sea
from drains, the creeks, the gully
guiding salmon back home

This morning a clear blue sky
a chickadee world

Over the rooftops
more geese going south
looking for a warm memory

Bare trees
the wind misses
the swish of leaves

Morning light, clear sky
a line of snow geese
sparking like diamonds

Almost unnoticed
a deer stands on the lawn
like a FOR RENT sign

Against the sky
a clown horn rusted
to a snow goose wing

Geese in a line
interrupting
a jet contrail

Wet streets, raining, walking by
the clean smell of a laundry

A wet penny
holding to the tar
like a limpet

It passes
very slowly
the worm subway

He stops me on the curb,
"Guess who got evicted?
Yours truly."

A deer with horns
headed for the tall weeds
beyond the fence

Two crows on the black car
clicking camera eyes

Cautiously
the dream animals
start to appear

Where I can't see
the ocean must be
reflecting blue sky

Mornings like this
when even the geese
go the wrong way

I have one minute left
the clock is ticking
it's almost time

We could be fish
these are the fins we use
to put on raincoats

Through the overflowing creek
the dog runs back and forth
crazy fried-egg eyes

Rain creates all these new rivers

A chicken coop
with electricity and
a hen in the window

Morning time
lead your own parade

Enough swans
to form a horn
in the air

I'm walking
where flowers
will grow

The distance it takes
to walk eating an apple
stays about the same

In the woods
an owl brushes
the night air

The cold
makes itself at home
settling in

Ice in patches
sewn to the ground
where puddles were

New orange light
in the chicken house
like an oven

People
I see once
and never again

Christmas
along the fence
lights shine

Memory moth
go where you're needed
bring what they forgot

Outside
the quiet street
snowlight

First snow
uncomfortable
stuck to grass

I have worn
a path in the grass
going to work

The same path
a little different
every day

A RED LEAF BOAT
Written in Fall 2021

From *Homeless Sutra* (2018)

Books by Good Deed Rain

Saint Lemonade, Allen Frost, 2014. Two novels illustrated by the author in the manner of the old Big Little Books.

Playground, Allen Frost, 2014. Poems collected from seven years of chapbooks.

Roosevelt, Allen Frost, 2015. A Pacific Northwest novel set in July, 1942, when a boy and a girl search for a missing elephant. Illustrated throughout by Fred Sodt.

5 Novels, Allen Frost, 2015. Novels written over five years, featuring circus giants, clockwork animals, detectives and time travelers.

The Sylvan Moore Show, Allen Frost, 2015. A short story omnibus of 193 stories written over 30 years.

Town in a Cloud, Allen Frost, 2015. A three-part book of poetry, written during the Bellingham rainy seasons of fall, winter, and spring.

A Flutter of Birds Passing Through Heaven: A Tribute to Robert Sund, 2016. Edited by Allen Frost and Paul Piper. The story of a legendary Ish River poet & artist.

At the Edge of America, Allen Frost, 2016. Two novels in one book blend time travel in a mythical poetic America.

Lake Erie Submarine, Allen Frost, 2016. A two week vacation in Ohio inspired these poems, illustrated by the author.

and Light, Paul Piper, 2016. Poetry written over three years. Illustrated with watercolors by Penny Piper.

The Book of Ticks, Allen Frost, 2017. A giant collection of 8 mysterious adventures featuring Phil Ticks. Illustrated throughout by Aaron Gunderson.

I Can Only Imagine, Allen Frost, 2017. Five adventures of love and heartbreak dreamed in an imaginary world. Cover & color illustrations by Annabelle Barrett.

The Orphanage of Abandoned Teenagers, Allen Frost, 2017. A fictional guide for teens and their parents. Illustrated by the author.

In the Valley of Mystic Light: An Oral History of the Skagit Valley Arts Scene, 2017. A comprehensive illustrated tribute. Edited by Claire Swedberg & Rita Hupy.

Different Planet, Allen Frost, 2017. Four science fiction adventures: reincarnation, robots, talking animals, outer space and clones. Illustrated by Laura Vasyutynska.

Go with the Flow: A Tribute to Clyde Sanborn, 2018. Edited by Allen Frost. The life and art of a timeless river poet. In beautiful living color!

Homeless Sutra, Allen Frost, 2018. Four stories: Sylvan Moore, a flying monk, a water salesman, and a guardian rabbit.

The Lake Walker, Allen Frost 2018. A little novel set in black and white like one of those old European movies about death and life.

A Hundred Dreams Ago, Allen Frost, 2018. A winter book of poetry and prose. Illustrated by Aaron Gunderson.

Almost Animals, Allen Frost, 2018. A collection of linked stories, thinking about what makes us animals.

The Robotic Age, Allen Frost, 2018. A vaudeville magician and his faithful robot track down ghosts. Illustrated throughout by Aaron Gunderson.

Kennedy, Allen Frost, 2018. This sequel to *Roosevelt* is a coming-of-age fable set during two weeks in 1962 in a mythical Kennedyland. Illustrated throughout by Fred Sodt.

Fable, Allen Frost, 2018. There's something going on in this country and I can best relate it in fable: the parable of the rabbits, a bedtime story, and the diary of our trip to Ohio.

Elbows & Knees: Essays & Plays, Allen Frost, 2018. A thrilling collection of writing about some of my favorite subjects, from B-movies to Brautigan.

The Last Paper Stars, Allen Frost 2019. A trip back in time to the 20 year old mind of Frankenstein, and two other worlds of the future.

Walt Amherst is Awake, Allen Frost, 2019. The dreamlife of an office worker. Illustrated throughout by Aaron Gunderson.

When You Smile You Let in Light, Allen Frost, 2019. An atomic love story written by a 23 year old.

Pinocchio in America, Allen Frost, 2019. After 82 years buried underground, Pinocchio returns to life behind a car repair shop in America.

164

Taking Her Sides on Immortality, Robert Huff, 2019. The long awaited poetry collection from a local, nationally renowned master of words.

Florida, Allen Frost, 2019. Three days in Florida turned into a book of sunshine inspired stories.

Blue Anthem Wailing, Allen Frost, 2019. My first novel written in college is an apocalyptic, Old Testament race through American shadows while Amelia Earhart flies overhead.

The Welfare Office, Allen Frost, 2019. The animals go in and out of the office, leaving these stories as footprints.

Island Air, Allen Frost, 2019. A detective novel featuring haiku, a lost library book and streetsongs.

Imaginary Someone, Allen Frost, 2020. A fictional memoir featuring 45 years of inspirations and obstacles in the life of a writer.

Violet of the Silent Movies, Allen Frost, 2020. A collection of starry-eyed short story poems, illustrated by the author.

The Tin Can Telephone, Allen Frost, 2020. A childhood memory novel set in 1975 Seattle, illustrated by author.

Heaven Crayon, Allen Frost, 2020. How the author's first book *Ohio Trio* would look if printed as a Big Little Book. Illustrated by the author.

Old Salt, Allen Frost, 2020. Authors of a fake novel get chased by tigers. Illustrations by the author.

A Field of Cabbages, Allen Frost, 2020. The sequel to *The Robotic Age* finds our heroes in a race against time to save Sunny Jim's ghost. Illustrated by Aaron Gunderson.

River Road, Allen Frost, 2020. A paperboy delivers the news to a ghost town. Illustrated by the author.

The Puttering Marvel, Allen Frost, 2021. Eleven short stories with illustrations by the author.

Something Bright, Allen Frost, 2021. 106 short story poems walking with you from winter into spring. Illustrated by the author.

The Trillium Witch, Allen Frost, 2021. A detective novel about witches in the Pacific Northwest rain. Illustrated by the author.

Cosmonaut, Allen Frost, 2021. Yuri Gagarin's rocket lands in America. Midnight jazz, folk music, mystery and sorcery. Illustrated by the author.

Thriftstore Madonna, Allen Frost, 2021. 124 summer story poems. Illustrated by the author.

Half a Giraffe, Allen Frost, 2021. A magical novel about a counterfeiter and his unusual, beloved pet. Illustrated by the author.

Lexington Brown & The Pond Projector, Allen Frost, 2022. An underwater invention takes three friends through time. Illustrated by Aaron Gunderson.

The Robert Huck Museum, Allen Frost, 2022. The artist's life story told in photographs, woodcuts, paintings, prints and drawings.

Mrs. Magnusson & Friends, Allen Frost, 2022. A collection of 13 stories featuring mystery and ginkgo leaves.

Magic Island, Allen Frost, 2022. There's a memory machine in this magical novel that takes us to college.

A Red Leaf Boat, Allen Frost, 2022. Inspired by Japan, this book of poems is the result of walking in autumn.

CPSIA information can be obtained
at www.ICGtesting.com
Printed in the USA
BVHW071955281022
650563BV00015B/1447